MARRY IN HASTE

15 Short Stories of Dating, Love and Marriage

DEBBIE YOUNG

Dedication

"What do you mean, your parents never argue?" My high school English teacher was sceptical that two people could form a lifelong bond without falling out along the way. "They must wait until you're out of the room and do it then."

This book is dedicated to my parents, former childhood sweethearts. After celebrating more than sixty wedding anniversaries together, they are still the best advertisement for marriage that I know.

Contents

PART I

SEEKING

1

The Real Thing

The black plastic cafeteria tray was still damp as Jackie set it down on the servery rail. As she dried her hands on her skirt, she glanced up at the day's Specials board.

"Special" was a generous adjective to apply to the mass-produced dishes reheated in the cafeteria kitchen. But there was one item on the menu that had recently become truly special to Jackie, and that was Chicken Korma.

Until a month ago, Jackie had never tried Indian food. Then came that memorable lunchtime when she realised that Mitesh Prawani, who usually dined in the later lunch break, was standing immediately in front of her in the queue. She'd admired Mitesh from afar since she'd spotted him entering the executive lift on his first day at Blofeld Insurance. Until that fateful lunch hour, though, it wasn't just the company lifts policy that had kept them apart, nor their different lunch shifts, but four thick concrete floors.

Mitesh worked on Level Six in Financial Management, while Jackie was rooted in Level Two's

Call Centre. The internal mailman had helped Jackie deduce that Mitesh's desk lay immediately over hers. In the Call Centre's rare quiet moments, she'd gaze up at the ceiling, imagining Mitesh poised above her.

"What do you fancy?" he turned to ask her with a smile, nudging her tray with his. She blushed, thinking for a moment that he'd said not "what" but "who".

"I'd skip the Chicken Korma, if I were you," he continued across her silence. "It's nothing like the real thing."

"Isn't it?" she answered faintly. "I wouldn't know. I've never had it."

His mouth fell open. "Never had proper Chicken Korma? Sweetheart, you don't know what you're missing! Rich, smooth, luscious, subtly spiced."

She managed not to voice what popped up in her head: "Just like you".

As soon as Jackie had collected her shepherd's pie, Mitesh beckoned her to share his table. When he invited her to join him for dinner that night at an authentic Indian restaurant, she nearly choked on the gristle she'd been valiantly chewing. She was too shy to do anything as intimate as spit it out and put it on the side of her plate in front of him.

So began Jackie's month of discovering the joys of traditional Indian food, but more than any spice, Mitesh's presence made her tingle from her taste buds to her toes.

When Mitesh eventually dumped her in favour of Accounts Receivable's Stacey (as he advised her in a note in the internal mail), Jackie swore she'd never eat Indian food again. Cloves, cumin, coriander – these once-loved spices would forever be bitter as bile.

But now, as she dithered once more before the Specials board, Jackie felt a hand placed gently on her shoulder. Turning round, she saw it belonged to Hu Chang, manager of Blofeld's corporate fleet.

"I wouldn't risk the sweet and sour chicken, love," he said. "It's nothing like the real thing – not like The Golden Sun's in town."

"Really?" replied Jackie, whose personal sun had just emerged from behind a dark cloud. "I've never had proper Chinese food before…"

2

Housetraining Thomas

As Clare checked her watch in the dim light of the *Belle Epoque* bistro, she wondered not for the first time how she and Joanna had managed to remain firm friends since they'd left school. On paper, they were completely incompatible; different people in just about every respect.

Whenever they met for a lunch date, Clare was always on time, and often early. When Joanna finally arrived, she'd fling open the door, dramatically exclaiming excuses for her lateness, not caring how many heads turned in her direction.

Clare always dressed in colour-coordinated outfits, neatly accessorised. Her well-organised purse, in which the Queen on the banknotes was facing the front and the right way up, contained valid credit and debit cards with plenty of capacity to cover her half of the lunch bill. She always had enough loose change for the tip.

Joanna, by contrast, looked as if she dressed in the first things that fell out of her wardrobe, and she often forgot to bring any money at all.

Each took the other to places they'd never otherwise visit. When it was Clare's turn to choose their meeting place, she'd pick a friendly, welcoming venue serving healthy food. Ideally it would be vegan or wholefood. Joanna would plump for whatever was trendy: sushi, Korean, Persian.

Clare preferred a dog-friendly café so that no-one would mind if she brought George, her perfectly-trained Yorkshire Terrier, in her capacious handbag. In some of the restaurants Joanna favoured, Clare suspected dogs were welcome only as menu items. She reached down now and patted George's head, glad he was on safe territory today.

Joanna, more of a cat person, never took much notice of Clare's dog. She secretly regarded George as a poor substitute for the ideal man that Clare had yet to find. Joanna was never short of men. It wasn't that she was promiscuous, just serially monogamous. She favoured a substandard boyfriend over single status, no contest.

"He'll do for now," Joanna often said to Clare about her latest squeeze. Clare thought her friend treated men like the free hire cars that garages supply. While your own vehicle is being restored after a crash they are preferable to walking, but they're never as comfortable or familiar.

Clare preferred to hold out for Mr Right. "Patience is a virtue," she'd declare, sure that her system was the best route to a long and happy marriage.

Joanna disagreed.

Clare was just reminding herself that they'd both assumed they'd be married by the age they were now when Joanna breezed in, swooping on the pre-lunch glass of Prosecco that her friend had waiting for her.

Before long they fell to discussing their dating status. Clare went first, reporting, as usual, a nil return.

"You're too selective, that's your trouble," said Joanna. "Too demanding. By saying you're only ever prepared to hitch up with a vegan, you narrow your chances of ever finding anyone. Supposing Benedict Cumberbatch walked in the door right now and proposed? Would you turn him down because he eats meat?"

Joanna didn't wait for Clare's answer.

"Sometimes, good enough is good enough. And besides, if you found someone absolutely perfect, it would be impossible to live up to their standards. You'd have to be perfect too."

Her lecture continued until their main course was ready. They sat back to allow the waiter, a slender Frenchman, to place their main courses in front of them – vegetable risotto for Clare, *steak frites* for Joanna. Clare focused on her own plate to avoid seeing Joanna's meat and hijacked the interruption as a prompt to reverse their roles.

"So how are things with you, then?" she asked, toying with a spear of asparagus.

"Well," Joanna began, "I've been doing my best since Thomas moved in, but I have to say I'm feeling a little unsettled at the moment."

Clare frowned. Last time they'd met, it had been all about Simon. He must have exited Joanna's love life as quickly as he'd entered. Why could Joanna not see that dating one leading man would be more satisfying than working her way through the chorus?

"When I first set eyes on Thomas, I thought he was lovely. I knew he'd end up coming home with me to stay."

"So he did?"

It's like catching repeats of *Poirot* on the telly, thought Clare. You know how they're going to end, but you sit and watch them anyway. While Joanna chattered on, Clare concentrated on rearranging the asparagus tips in her risotto to point north.

"When I first brought him back to mine, it felt as if he'd always been there. He seemed right at home. The weather was atrocious, cold and wet. Do you remember those storms around the bank holiday weekend? We curled up on the sofa together under blankets for a movie marathon. Romantic black and white films with the lights down. Bliss! But once I was back at work, I realised I'd made a mistake. He is so demanding. He expects me to give him his dinner the minute I get home, complaining how hungry he is before I even get my coat off. I get no peace or space to do anything for myself. He just wants me paying attention to him the whole evening."

Joanna held out her hands, palms down, for Clare to examine.

"Is it any wonder my nails are in such a state? I haven't had a chance for a proper manicure since he moved in."

"Doesn't Thomas have a job to go to?" Clare ventured, hoping Thomas wasn't another long-haired hippy like Merlin, whom Joanna had met at a funfair. He had absconded with her jewellery box after a week – but at least he had been a vegan.

Joanna laid down her knife and fork and looked at Clare levelly.

"A job? I can't imagine what kind of job a cat might do. A model, maybe? Cosmetics tester? Really, Clare, you do have some strange ideas sometimes."

"So, Thomas is a cat? You've got a new cat? Is that what you've been on about?"

Joanna finished her Prosecco and looked around the café, waving the empty glass as a hint for a refill.

"Yes, of course, whatever did you think he was? An elephant? Now, where's that gorgeous waiter got to?" said Joanna, with a sly smile that hinted at more than thirst.

3

Old Flames, New Sparks

"So tell me, are you still as gorgeous and loveable as you were ten years ago?"

My first instinct is to say yes, in reply to Andrew Turner's unexpected email message, which has just arrived in my inbox beneath the subject line "Old Flames".

A superficial observer might agree with me. I'm slimmer, better groomed and more stylishly dressed than when I left my parents' farm for university. The salary from my subsequent job as a sales executive in the city enables me to buy more expensive clothes too.

But I'm not sure I feel as loveable. You see, it's been nearly a year since I split up with Stephen, and, to use a good agricultural phrase, I've been lying fallow a little too long. That doesn't do a girl any good. I've started to let myself go.

I'm spared from wondering how Andrew Turner has fared by comparison because his email goes on to tell me. He is now a successful accountant. This career choice is no surprise: he won the prize for being first in our primary school class to know all his times tables.

That's when I started to go off him.

After we went our separate ways to single-sex high schools in the nearest town, we'd occasionally spot each other in the local shop or pub, but that was as far as our relationship went.

He is back living in the village, which demonstrates he's earning a good salary. Hardly any of our generation can afford to buy houses there, and no rental properties are available, so the rest of us have had to move away.

My trips home are few and far between, confined to Christmas, Easter, family birthdays and the odd week in the summer when my leave from work outstrips my holiday budget. To be honest, after living away for nearly a decade, going back makes me feel like a fish out of water. I couldn't even bring myself to return for our primary school's hundredth birthday party a few months ago. I had been fond of the school, but I didn't want to draw attention to my single status fifteen years after I'd left it. To salve my conscience, I added my email address to its alumni database.

I realise with a start that I haven't seen Andrew Turner for over a decade. I wonder whether I'd still recognise him.

I don't need to wonder for long, because he's attached a recent photo of himself. He looks smart standing at a lectern in a dark suit, an out-of-focus graph on the screen behind him. He is leaning forward, smiling confidently as if he's just cracked a clever gag to a wildly receptive audience. On his left hand, curled around a bulbous microphone, there is no wedding ring.

He looks successful. He looks affluent.

I focus on his face, trying to spot the difference between this grown-up image and my memory of him as a teenager. Suddenly I remember my mother saying

"Young Andrew Turner will be a heartbreaker when he grows up", but at ten years old I could never see beyond the scruffy home haircut, bad complexion and smugness about his times tables.

Now I can. An expensive hairdresser has tamed his curls, his skin has cleared to a healthy glow beneath the stage spotlights, and his blue eyes suggest the power to melt any woman's resistance.

My answer to his question will, of course, be yes. I scrabble about my hard drive to find a flattering self-portrait to send him. The only work shots I have make me look excruciatingly bored, as if there against my will, which is accurate enough. I raid the folder of my holiday snaps, and choose one in which I'm lounging in a bikini besides Polly, my best friend from uni, on a girls-only trip to Majorca. We look healthy and happy, despite our hangovers.

Before attaching it to my message, I crop out Polly. This is no time to field competition.

I compose my reply to be no longer than Andrew Turner's message. I don't want to look desperate, so I am selective with the truth.

"Yes, I am as gorgeous and lovable as ever, living the young, free and single high life in the Big Smoke. I'm kept busy by my responsible job, in which I've recently been promoted to Senior Sales Executive." He needn't know at this stage that what I sell is cheap plastic toys imported from China, that I work in a call centre, or that the Senior title signifies only that I've survived a year without punching my boss or insulting a customer. Nor do I reveal that my flat, which is actually only a bedsit, is rented, not owned.

As I hit "reply", I notice he's sweetly put "Old Flames" in the address field instead of my name. That's rather overstating the case, since the only time we ever so much as embraced was in a playground game of kiss chase when we were about seven years old. My message disappears into cyberspace, and I shut down my email dashboard, nurturing a funny feeling that a reply will appear before long.

As I change into my pyjamas ready for bed, I allow myself to wallow in memories, apparently stashed away in the depths of my subconscious for all these years. Perhaps I always knew that our relationship might blossom eventually.

Andrew Turner had sat next to me in Year 5. That year, he gave me a chocolate selection box as a Christmas present. It was the cheapest kind, with a Fudge bar and a Milky Way rather than Mars Bars and Crunchies, but I was delighted. In gratitude, I gave him a chaste Christmas kiss on the cheek.

It would seem I was wrong about the last time being when we were seven.

I clean my teeth, remembering that on our last day at primary school, Andrew Turner was the only boy to add kisses to his scrawled signature on my shirt. That has to be significant. I'm so flattered to think he's been carrying a torch for me all these years, I'm even prepared to forgive him for winning the coveted times tables prize. Maybe one day our child will follow in his footsteps and win that very same prize.

As I begin to floss, more carefully than usual now that I've got a man back in my life, I realise where I've been going wrong with my string of failed relationships: I've been looking too far from home. The perfect match would be someone who shares my rural background and culture; someone who values community rather than the distant reserve of city life.

To find a husband in my village would be like a homecoming. I wonder why I've never thought of Andrew Turner in that way before.

I spit into the sink and turn on the tap to wash the flecks of toothpaste down the plughole.

Next day at work, I realise to my horror that I've left my mobile phone at home. It's a sackable offence to check my personal email messages at work, so I'm on tenterhooks till the end of the day.

I'm taking it for granted that there will be a reply. As a professional accountant, Andrew Turner will be allowed to send personal emails at the office. On reading my response, he will surely ask me out. We've wasted too much time already.

I fumble for the front door key, as nervous as if Andrew Turner was inside waiting for me, throw my bag on the sofa and grab my phone from the coffee table to access my emails.

It's there all right: a new message from Andrew Turner, with "New Sparks" in the subject line. I click on it greedily. It's short, like his first email, but I put this down to him being a man of numbers rather than letters.

"That's all good, sweetheart. How about meeting for a drink to talk about old times – and the new times ahead? Let's not visit The Eagle" – that's our village pub – "where we'd be distracted by everyone who knows us. How about The Bluebird instead? Axxx"

The Bluebird is the pub in the small town where we went to our respective secondary schools. The pupils of both the boys' and the girls' high schools aspired to get served at The Bluebird as soon as we thought we could pass for eighteen.

For a moment, it strikes me as odd that Andrew Turner hasn't suggested meeting at a halfway point between our homes. Reading, for example, would be ideal. But then I decide it's more romantic to rekindle our relationship in this significant old haunt – on common cultural ground, you might say.

I'm basking in memories of teenage trips to The Bluebird, trying in vain to recollect one featuring Andrew Turner, when a new message pings into my inbox. By a strange coincidence, this one's from another old school friend, Amy Williams, now a paediatric doctor in Scotland.

"The Bluebird?" her message begins with no salutation. "Are you mad? You were never much cop at geography, Andrew, but do you have no idea how long it would take me to drive down from Dumfries? I hope you're not assuming I'd stay the night with you. LOL."

I read her email again, unable to make sense of it. Scrolling down to see how many letters she has after her name these days, I notice her email is the reply to a message from Andrew Turner. Word for word, it's the same as the second one he sent to me:

"That's all good, sweetheart…"

It's preceded by her response to his first message (also the same as mine). Only her reply differs: "Andrew, how lovely to hear from you. Always good to catch up with old friends. Sorry to hear from my parents that you lost your job and are living back at home with your mum. Still, I'm sure another job will come along soon. There's always going to be a need for accounts clerks. Luv Amy xxx"

I stare, open-mouthed. Has Andrew Turner emailed all the girls in our year? Curse that school alumni database! Maybe he reasoned that he'd hit the jackpot with at least one of us if he tried us all. Did he think we'd be easily impressed just because he once won a times tables prize? Amy Williams, always a smart cookie, saw straight through him from the start. For the first time, I realise that his emails contain no personalised content – not even my name. As if any of us could ever be described as his "old flame"!

Now Amy's beaten him at his own game, copying her reply to the rest of the girls in our class.

Stupid boy, he should have done what all the rest of us did and looked further afield. There's no chance of finding a soul-mate in a small village community. When you've grown up like brother and sister, marrying would feel like incest.

I return to the email he's just sent me. The correct reply to this one is as obvious as it was to his first one:

"Dear Andrew

Get a life. The rest of us have, haven't we, girls?"

But I don't send it. I'm not that mean. I simply click "delete" on the whole thread, remove him and his smarmy Photoshopped picture from my contacts list, and block him.

Instead I determine to make the most of my time between boyfriends. Like London buses, another one will turn up soon. I just need to stop checking the timetable, looking at my watch, and staring at the horizon while I'm waiting.

4

The Matchmaker

As I enter the overheated waiting room, I remove my dark glasses and turn down the collar of my coat. If I try to maintain my disguise in this atmosphere, I'll keel over.

No matter. At least I'm off the street now, and unlikely to be recognised by anyone I know. I assume the staff here must adhere to some kind of client confidentiality rule, as at an STD clinic. Not that I've ever visited one of those, you understand.

Gazing warily across the room at me is the only other client waiting: an olive-skinned chap with glossy dark hair. He's of no interest to me. I put on my form that I prefer blue-eyed blonds.

"Your first time here?" he asks with a sympathetic twinkle in his eye. "Don't worry, I'm sure it won't be as bad as you think. It's not like it's an STD clinic."

I gasp, blushing at how easily he's read my mind. He laughs aloud. "Sorry! Forgive a medic's bluntness. I didn't mean to make you feel awkward. It's bad enough that we have to resort to a dating agency without me adding to your suffering. I'm Ahmed, by the way. I'm a doctor."

"Paula," I say, sitting down a carefully calculated two seats away from him. I'm happy to chat, and he seems nice enough, but in a room with ten chairs, it would seem pushy to sit right next to him. "You're right, it is my first time here, and I am a bit nervous. I don't want any of my clients to see me. It diminishes my credibility as a family lawyer to admit single status."

He smiles wryly, and his eyes crinkle at the corners. I notice how dark they are, almost black.

"So, a fellow professional, eh? What is it about us high achievers that makes us so hopeless on the dating front?"

I shrug. "Fear of a messy divorce, in my case – I've seen too many of them at work. But surely that doesn't apply to medics. Don't you have nurses fawning all over you and grateful patients proposing marriage, or does that only happen in films?"

"Yes, if you're something glamorous like a heart surgeon. Anaesthetists like me don't have the same appeal."

I think for a moment. "When I had my appendix out, the anaesthetist was lovely. He held my hand as I fell asleep. Listening to him count backwards in his soft Welsh accent was very soothing."

"Yes, but I bet you never saw him again afterwards. No further opportunity to connect."

I shook my head. "No, I hadn't thought of that. In fact, I'd forgotten all about him until now. I put him out of my mind along with the trauma of the operation."

"Exactly. And in any case, what do you think it does to a guy's ego when every girl whose hand he holds passes out and has to be wheeled away on a stretcher for someone else to have their way with her?"

I clap my hand over my mouth to suppress a laugh at his misfortune.

"But surely you don't have that problem with the nurses?"

He shakes his head slowly, warily. "No, but you'd be surprised at how many of them steer clear of me. Knowing that at work I have the power of life and death puts them off. Either that or they think I go around with a pocketful of knock-out drugs, and I'm not afraid to use them. But I'm just an ordinary bloke at the end of the day, once I take off my green mask."

"Now that does sound creepy. At least I don't have to wear a mask for my job. Nor even a white wig."

He scans me with a twinkle in his dark eyes. "I don't know, I've always had a penchant for older women."

He doesn't need to resort to anaesthetics to make me relax.

Suddenly a secretary puts her head round the waiting room door.

"Ahmed, would you go through the red door, please? Sally is ready for you now."

She indicates two doors, one scarlet, one pink, at the far end of the room.

"She makes it sound like a brothel," he whispers to me as he gets up from his chair. "Nice meeting you, Paula."

"Nice meeting you too, Doctor. Good luck! I hope they find someone for you."

Once he's closed the door behind him, I hear his conversation with Sally, the dating counsellor, but I can't make out what they're saying. By way of distraction, I seize the folder of case studies nestling on the coffee table between bridal magazines and holiday brochures. Seeking hope in its pages of cheesy wedding snaps from satisfied clients, I wonder whether they remove the photos of those who subsequently divorce.

Ten minutes later, the secretary reappears to direct me to the pink door. I'm to be quizzed by Julie, a middle-aged woman wearing too much make-up. Her generously applied perfume forces me to sit back in my chair, but Julie is sympathetic, kindly and supportive. Her compassionate attitude confirms my decision to consult a dating agency run by human beings rather than computer algorithms. No computer software could ever replace a thinking breathing being with a heart and a brain.

Julie asks me a surprising number of searching questions about all aspects of my life, such as which position I'd preferred in school netball games and the name of my first pet. I make a mental note to change my security question for my online back account the minute I get home. She's long on questions, but short on answers. Eventually I feel it must be my turn to do the asking.

So, taking all the evidence into account," I begin, "do you have anyone on your books who'd be a good match for me?"

I picture myself, all in white, in the coffee table photo album, trying to imagine the man in a suit beside me.

Julie reaches across the desk to pat my hand reassuringly.

"All in good time. I'm sure we'll find someone for you. I hope you weren't expecting an instant result today. We don't deliver our verdict on the spot. The jury must retire to consider its verdict."

She picks up her paperweight (a red rose trapped, airless, in solid resin) and bangs it on the desk, like a judge's gavel. "Court dismissed!"

She looks pleased with herself at entering into what she perceives to be my world. Her chuckle dissipates as she spots my pursed lips, and she starts shuffling my paperwork into a pink manila file.

"So, all done for today. We'll be in touch again within forty-eight hours. We just need to feed all this lovely data into our computer to see what it comes up with."

At the mention of the computer, my heart sinks – not the effect a dating agency wants to create. I might as well have stuck to the internet agencies in the privacy of my own home.

"Thanks anyway, Julie," I say, trying to sound grateful as I gather up my coat and briefcase ready to leave. After all, she's been kind enough, and she's only doing her job. She's just not the Fairy Godmother I was hoping for.

She ushers me out through a different door which opens into the alley running down the side of the building to the High Street. It must be the post-consultation exit to avoid clients airing their disillusionment to anyone still in the waiting room.

The drizzle outside might as well be a bucket of cold water. My hopes of instant romance dashed, I don my dark glasses and shrug on my raincoat. As I near the end of the alley, a flurry of footsteps behind me makes me clutch my briefcase in both hands ready to fend off a mugger.

Then a man's hand clamps onto my shoulder with a firm yet unaggressive touch. I spin round to find myself gazing up at a familiar pair of dark eyes.

"Might I prescribe a painkilling glass of *vino* in the bistro across the road? If your interview was anything like mine, you'll be feeling the need."

I lower my shades and nod. As Ahmed and I turn onto the high street, I smile into the early evening sunshine.

"Thank you, Doctor, that's fine by me. I promise I won't pass out and have to be wheeled away."

"And I won't sue you if you do."

As he takes my hand with the confident grip of one used to daily physical contact with strangers, I hope we're both telling the truth.

5

The Homecoming

"Oh my God, Harry, you've been burgled!" Suki stands rigid in the doorway, refusing to follow me across the threshold.

"Whatever makes you think that?" I dump my backpack on the couch. She waves her hands to indicate the whole room before her.

"But nothing's missing." I pat the open laptop on the coffee table and the teetering pile of CDs behind it. "Look, all this stuff's exactly where I left it. I'd been burning tracks on to my iPod. That laptop's brand new. No burglar would have left that behind."

I point to the pile of coins on my desk. "Rank amateurs if they couldn't spot ready cash."

I wink at her in hope of lightening her mood, guessing she's tired and irrational after the delayed flight home from Ibiza, but she remains in the doorway, as if rooted by her silver wheeled suitcase. I prise the handle out of her clenched hand. She follows me into the room.

"Mind where you put it!"

"What? You left it in the hands of baggage handlers for the last few hundred miles, yet you don't trust me to move it a few metres?"

"It's just that – it's new, and I don't want to get it dirty."

Definitely irrational. Suki sits down gingerly on the edge of the sofa, looking like she's waiting for a job interview.

"I think what you need is a nice cup of tea, sweetheart. Reacclimatise you to British soil after our holiday. It was a fabulous holiday, wasn't it?"

I perch next to Suki for a moment and run my hand reassuringly down her spine. Her white vest is a bit flimsy for British weather, and the back of her neck looks pinker than when we boarded the plane home. She must have got a bit sunburnt on that last long, lazy day on the beach.

"I'll get you that cuppa, sweetheart."

I top up the kettle, flick down the switch, grab two cups from the washing-up bowl and swish them under the running tap. As the kettle starts to steam, I fetch the milk from the fridge. The fumes from the carton make me cough.

"Is black tea okay, or black coffee? I think the milk's gone off."

"Gone off? I should think it would be cheese by now if it's been there since before we went away!"

I shrug. I wouldn't have noticed if she hadn't said. "I'll nip out to Sainsbury's in a bit to get some fresh. You staying to supper?"

I shake some instant coffee out of the jar into each mug and pour on the water. Unable to find a clean spoon, I swirl the mugs around to dissolve the granules as I take them back into the living room.

"We've had such a lovely time, I don't want you to go." Sitting next to Suki on the sofa, I sense her relax slightly so I press my thigh against hers. "It's not as if we've got work tomorrow. Let's add an extra day to our holiday, finish it off together here at my flat, shall we?"

Bizarrely, it will be the first night she's spent at my flat. Until now she's only ever popped in occasionally; somehow we've always ended up at hers after a date. Well, I say somehow – the first time she invited me in, I realised how much nicer her place was than mine: clean sheets, lots of pillows, posh toiletries lined up neatly in the bathroom. It was like staying at a hotel. There was even the daily paper folded neatly on the coffee table, alongside a bowl of dried flower petals. It always seems odd to me, using something dead to scent a room, but I'm willing to accept that little foible as the rest of the flat is so comfy.

I know she's been worried about her lease running out not long after our holiday, just as her new teaching term is due to start. I loop my arm around her shoulders and lean her back against the sofa.

"Actually, I've been thinking while we were away. I mean, we got on so well, didn't we? Don't we have fun together?"

Suki snuggles back, against me rather than the sofa. "It was perfect. That gorgeous hotel with its private beach, and the room service and the maids." She closes her eyes and rests her head on my shoulder.

"Exactly. So why don't you move in here with me now we're back? It would be much less hassle than hunting for a new place. Our holiday doesn't have to end just because we've come home."

Suki's eyes shoot open. "What, here?" She sits forward in her seat again and surveys my flat, as if considering how to rate it out of ten. "Well, don't take this the wrong way, but I think it might need a bit of work on it first."

"You reckon? I can fix the net curtain rail, if you like. And I'll line those carpet tiles up again properly."

I nudge one with the toe of my trainer to fit it back into place. I've always been fond of these carpet tiles. It's a bit like having a giant jigsaw on the floor.

"Blinds would be better than nets, and how about laminate flooring and a rug? Much easier to keep clean and tidy." Suki pats the hard arm of the sofa. "And cushions. I can't believe you haven't got any scatter cushions!" She gives a little laugh, and I'm glad she's cheering up. "I know! When we go to Sainsbury's for the milk, let's stock up on cleaning materials – I don't suppose you've got any of those?"

She looks around and finds no shortage of evidence to confirm her suspicion.

"I've got a washing-up sponge."

She shakes her head. "I'll make a list. And tomorrow we can pop into IKEA and buy some Billy bookcases, and maybe some scented candles."

She claps her hands as if bringing her class to order, suddenly animated after her post-flight torpor. "Oh, Harry, this is so exciting! Thank you so much. I've been dreading having to start flat-hunting again. Though this will be a different kind of challenge."

I raise my eyebrows in surprise. All the women I've brought home before have hated housework. Some even broke up with me the minute they saw my bathroom.

I begin to think about the stuff Suki will be importing from her old flat. I hope she'll bring her panini machine. I've never achieved the same effect on sandwiches with my toaster, even though it works a treat on potato waffles. I don't even mind if she brings her bowl of dead flower petals. I think they'll look right at home here

PART II
COMMITTING

1

The Way to His Heart

Cindy decided to fall in love with Jack the moment he said, "Come back to my house". Yes, a house, not a bedsit or flat. Once she'd confirmed that he owned the property rather than renting it, she realised she'd finally found the man with whom she wanted to spend the rest of her life.

It was the sort of home that she could never have afforded to buy herself – not on her salary as a chef at the local pub where she and Jack had first met. Walking up the front path and spotting the beautiful stained glass panels framing the front door, she pictured herself being carried over the threshold one day, wearing a long white dress.

The frequency with which Jack dined in the pub made her realise that there was one thing she could offer that was otherwise out of his reach: good home-cooked meals. When she had first visited his house one chilly January evening, she'd thought it odd that he'd invited her for a drink rather than a meal, but she soon discovered why.

As he chose a chilled bottle of wine, she remarked, glancing around the expensively fitted kitchen, "That's a smart drinks cooler, but where do you keep your real fridge? The one for food?"

He had looked puzzled. "What do you mean? This is the real fridge."

Apparently he was not in the habit of keeping food in the house, other than the inevitable bachelor fare. Tins of soup and beans lurked lonely in the otherwise empty larder. An ageing sliced loaf of white bread languished on the worktop. A huge bag of twenty-four packs of crisps lay open, ransacked, next to the kettle.

Having found Jack's Achilles heel, Cindy took aim.

"Blimey, she's a keeper!" said Jack's best mate Tony a few weeks later after a post-match supper at Jack's house. "This casserole is amazing."

Cindy was out of earshot in the kitchen, brewing fresh coffee in the new Nespresso machine – the latest pricey gadget to arrive in the house, courtesy of Jack's credit card. To save himself the trouble of reimbursing her every time she bought something new for his house, he'd given her his pin number.

Jack gave a smug grin. "Yep. Since Cindy moved in, it's been like having a personal chef. Or an *au pair* without any children. Or the nights off."

He frowned for a moment. It was the first time he'd formally acknowledged that Cindy had taken up residence.

Tony winked and nudged him indulgently. "Don't knock it, mate. You're onto a winner. Go with the flow! Now, what's for pudding?"

When the clocks changed after Easter, Cindy began to plan for al fresco dining on the patio she'd told Jack to install ready for the summer. Jack didn't mind the weekend trips to the garden centre. Lifting bags of gravel, paving slabs and stone troughs would count as extra football training.

He also appreciated the new high-tech sun-loungers that Cindy had ordered from a glossy shopping catalogue. These luxurious chairs provided the perfect place in which to digest the first sumptuous Sunday lunch from their new barbecue. The marinated wild salmon and baked bananas had been washed down by chilled *rosé* from his new wine-club subscription, thoughtfully taken out by Cindy on his behalf. The joining gift had been a silver ice-bucket that stood between them, chilling the remains of a second bottle.

"Do you know, they use the same technology for these chairs as in the space programme," said Cindy, remembering the advert that had seduced her. "They're meant to make you feel like you're floating in outer space, defying gravity."

Jack nodded lazily. Sated and sleepy, he was certainly vulnerable as an astronaut.

"This is bliss," he sighed, sipping from one of his new crystal wine glasses. "I could do this forever."

He didn't specify whether he meant the wine, the comfy chair, the sunshine, or the stomach full of good food, but Cindy chose her own interpretation.

"Oh, but Jack, you can. I feel the same way too."

Noticing his eyes were still closed, Cindy quietly pulled the *Sunday Times* supplement out from under her seat. She'd deliberately left it open at an advertisement for designer engagement rings. Extracting a pen and

Jack's credit card from the pocket of her jeans, she started to fill in the order form.

2

Presents Tense

"You can't put anything from that catalogue on our present list!" gasped Kimberley. "It'll be in the public domain, on our wedding website. My boss might see it. And yours. And our future children. It'll be there forever."

"Well, you did say to go for something we didn't already have."

Kimberley snatched the Anne Summers brochure from Stephen's hands and sat on it to render it inaccessible.

"Yes, but I meant things that people would actually want to buy us."

"I think my mates would be very happy to buy us anything from Anne Summers," said Stephen, picking up his beer glass from the coffee table and taking a swig. "Though they'd probably be after me for a borrow. Or a review."

"Ugh." Kimberley seized her iPad from beside her wine glass and fired it up. "Look, let's just set up a list at John Lewis, then everything will be respectable and straightforward. It'll make life easier for everyone."

Stephen folded his arms, swung one knee over the other and sat back in his new cream leather recliner.

"The whole thing's ridiculous, if you ask me. We don't need presents. We've been living together for over a year, we each had our own place before that, and we've already got so much. We should be chucking stuff out, not begging for more. If we want something, we can buy it ourselves." He slapped the sturdy arm of his chair for emphasis. "We're not poor."

Kimberley sighed. "That's not the point. People will want to buy us wedding presents. It's like sealing the deal of our marriage."

"What, 'with this toaster, I thee wed?'"

Kimberley shook her head briskly, as if dismissing a comment from a dim-witted child. "Don't you see? If we don't make a list, they'll buy us something hideous of their own choosing – like they do for Christmas and birthdays, but at much greater cost. Making a list will save us taking things back to the shops for a refund. In any case, we can only do that with presents that include gift receipts. And not at all for anything personalised."

Stephen heaved himself up to a standing position, made his way to the kitchen, and returned with another bottle of Waitrose Essentials beer. (They'd been economising to pay for the wedding themselves.)

"What's happened to your feminist principles, Kim? Because what you're talking about is effectively asking for a dowry."

Kimberley's eyes widened in horror as he continued mercilessly. "What's more, every time someone comes to visit, they'll expect to see whatever they bought us on display or in use. The house won't feel like our own any more. Every wedding guest will have a stake in it. It'll be more like a timeshare than a home."

"All the more reason to dispense with Anne Summers."

Kimberley wanted to top up her wine glass from the box of rosé in their huge aquamarine fridge, but didn't dare move from the sofa in case Stephen grabbed the catalogue again. Focusing instead on her iPad, she started to navigate to the John Lewis wedding list page, but diverted to read an email pop-up message. It was a quote for one of the honeymoon holidays she'd been researching earlier that day. The price was much higher than she'd expected.

"I know! Let's ask our guests to contribute to our honeymoon fund instead of buying gifts!"

Stephen frowned. "Doesn't that smack of those dreadful self-indulgent holidays that masquerade as charity fundraisers? You know the sort of thing: 'Walk the Great Wall of China in aid of homeless kittens'. It would be like seeking sponsorship for sex."

Kimberley threw her iPad down on the coffee table a little too hard, then flung herself dramatically back on the sofa with her hands over her face, peeking between her fingers to make sure she hadn't shattered the iPad screen.

"Oh, for God's sake, Stephen, get a grip! When you get married, you have to comply with certain conventions to keep everyone happy. Creating a wedding present list is not a big ask. Why are you being so bloody difficult about it?"

Stephen scowled into his fast-emptying glass, then set it down on the coffee table. Grabbing the television remote control, he waved it around for emphasis.

"How can you ask your Great Auntie Alice to spend her paltry pension on a wedding present when we can afford to buy ourselves luxuries like this fancy big telly?"

"Great Auntie Alice would be mortified if we said that to her."

"I'm not suggesting we say it to her in so many words. Just that we ask everyone, in a blanket message, not to buy us presents. Like they do at funerals: 'no flowers, by request'."

"Now you're comparing our wedding to a funeral? How could you, Stephen? This is meant to be the happiest day of our lives!"

With a sob, Kimberley seized from the coffee table a purple marble egg – a souvenir of their last trip to Italy – and flung it as hard as she could at her fiancé. When he stood aside to dodge the missile, it scored a bullseye on a china vase of red roses on the mantelpiece behind him. They both watched the vase arc across the room, spilling its contents over the television, which responded with a shower of sparks, a loud crackle and a puff of smoke.

Swivelling round to assess the damage, Stephen stumbled over the pile of wedding magazines and travel brochures on the kilim. In his haste to break his fall, he let the remote control fly out of his hands. At high speed it headed with the precision of a heat-seeking missile to the centre of the television screen, which promptly cracked like melting ice upon a pond.

Two sharp intakes of breath from either side of the coffee table were followed by a single hollow silence. With a long and rasping sigh, Kimberley scooped up her iPad and jabbed at it to bring up the John Lewis wedding list page.

"So, a new television set it is. I suppose all our friends and relations could club together."

Stephen nodded as he dropped the remote control into the wastepaper basket. He crossed the room to sit beside Kimberley on the sofa, draped one arm about her shoulders and pulled her closer to him.

"Yep, job done," he said quietly, kissing the top of her bowed head.

3

Having Your Cake

I think one of the many great things about organising your own wedding is that you get to do it exactly how you want it, rather than how the so-called experts prefer to operate. Plus, of course, you avoid their extortionate fees.

The wedding cake is a prime example. How many weddings have you been to where you've been served an unappetising slice of cake the size of a matchbox and smothered in rock-hard royal icing? Half the guests worry about breaking their teeth on it, and the other half fear the sugar rush for their kids.

Lots of people can't stand marzipan. They either pick it off and leave it on the side of their plate, or force-feed it to the one person on their table who likes it. Fruit cakes terrify those with nut allergies, and nauseate people like me who have never outgrown their childhood abhorrence of dried fruit.

As for my mum's suggestion that we should have a fruit cake and save the bottom layer for a christening cake, that's downright disgusting. That tradition must have been invented before "sell-by" dates.

So, here I am, all set to create my very own wedding cake design – the perfect accompaniment to our big day. I'm keeping the details a secret from Malcolm, my husband-to-be. In return, he's allowed one secret from me: our honeymoon destination, which he's responsible for booking. I know it's in Italy somewhere – we are both nuts about Italy – but I've no idea where. It's all very exciting.

First, let me tell you about the type of cake I'm going to make. My name's Victoria, so the choice is obvious. I've never met anyone who doesn't love a Victoria sponge. My married name will be Cooper, so I'm going to fill the cake not with jam, but with Cooper's Marmalade. That's quite a posh brand.

The accent colour for my dress is lavender, so I'm going to stir a few dried lavender flowers into the mix and scatter more over the marmalade between the many layers. I'll colour the butter icing pale lavender, and fleck it with more dried lavender flowers.

Yes, I did say many layers, because I'm going to make more than one Victoria sponge. There has to be enough cake to go around our seventy-three guests, so I'm going to pile five sandwich cakes on top of each other. I've ordered four sets of little plastic pillars to stack them all up. The design will be in the style of a conventional wedding cake, but much prettier: a romantic lavender tower.

Fortunately, I had my hen night a week before the wedding (I'm not taking any risks), so it doesn't matter that I spend the evening before our big day baking five pairs of sponge cakes. It's midnight before I start dripping the mauve colouring into the butter icing. My eyes grow tired as I work under the harsh fluorescent strip light in the kitchen.

Once I've sandwiched each pair of cakes together with marmalade and butter icing, I pop them into cardboard cake boxes, and stack all five in a plastic crate for ease of transport. I drop in a plastic bag of lavender flowers to sprinkle over the whole cake tower once it's assembled at the church hall tomorrow, plus the box of pillars to separate the layers. The pillars came in the post a few days ago, and I haven't bothered to take them out of the packaging so as to keep them neat and tidy.

I've briefed my sisters, Elizabeth and Anne, to assemble the cake in the hall just before we sit down to eat. Meanwhile, I'll be getting stuck into the sparkling wine at the top table, being called "Mrs" by everybody.

With all my baking tasks complete, I finally fall asleep in a relaxing lavender-scented bath, dreaming of the inevitable applause when my sisters bring out the perfect wedding cake.

As the delivery boys distribute armfuls of pizza boxes to our guests, seated at long tables in the church hall for our reception, I squeeze my new husband's hand with satisfaction. Everything's gone exactly to plan. Our friends Rosa and Giovanni at the local Italian takeaway have done us a terrific deal for seventy-three top-of-the-range pizzas, and serving it in the boxes will save us having to worry about washing up. The pizza smells delicious, the perfect overture to our Italian honeymoon. Well, who doesn't like pizza?

After a while, I notice guests fiddling with the little wedding favours that we've set in front of every place. Some people are wondering whether the Italian-style nets of pastel-coloured sugared almonds are meant to be pudding, so I signal to Elizabeth and Anne to bring out the cake. They exchange anxious glances before rising from their seats, and Anne detours on her way to the kitchen to whisper in my ear.

"Did you mean us to use all those little pillars? We've done it like you said, but there seemed to be an awful lot of them."

I give her a puzzled look. "If we used any fewer, the whole thing might collapse."

They shrug, and as they head through the kitchen door, I hear Elizabeth say to Anne, "Well, I still think four packets of sixteen is over the top."

The shiver that runs through me counteracts the warmth from the chillies on my pizza. I suddenly recall a moment of confusion when I ordered the pillars online. Were the prices given per pillar or pack of four? I'd thought the price per pillar was a bit high, but had clicked "buy now" anyway and hoped for the best.

My doubt is answered as Elizabeth emerges, bearing the cake aloft. Anne holds the door open for her before dutifully starting a round of applause.

Four of my five Victoria sponges are each resting on a circle of sixteen plastic columns, leaving barely any air space in between. So there must have been four lots of four in each pack after all.

As Elizabeth brings the cake to the top table and places it in front of my husband and me, to my horror I realise that the icing is not the subtle shade of lavender it had been last night under my kitchen lights, but a dirty grey. The dried lavender flowers look like grit, as if the cake's been accidentally dropped on the gravel path outside the hall.

My sisters raise their eyebrows as if to say "Are you sure about this?" then all but run back to their seats, abdicating responsibility for the cake to me.

Malcolm thumps the table to bring the murmuring room to silence, though the clapping has long since stopped. (He can't do the usual tap-on-the-glass-with-a-spoon trick because we're using paper cups to save washing up.) The reverberations have a dire effect on the cake. With glacial slowness it begins to sink down on the side nearest Malcolm. I reach out to stop it, but misjudge the pressure, and only the lower two tiers stabilise.

Not daring to take my eyes off the leaning cake, willing it not to collapse completely, I realise Malcolm is starting a second unscheduled speech.

"I already knew I was marrying a girl of many talents," he begins. I brace myself for a "but" which doesn't come. "As some of you will know, Victoria and I made a deal that we'd surprise each other on our wedding day. My surprise to her would be our honeymoon destination, and her surprise for me would be our wedding cake.

"I have to say, I never dreamed for a moment that these two would coincide so neatly. I don't believe my wife" – he pauses for the obligatory ripple of applause – "would start our marriage by cheating – surely she's not been secretly checking my laptop to see where I've booked our honeymoon, so I can only assume it is by some psychic power that she's detected our destination is Pisa. Reproducing its famous Leaning Tower in cake form is truly a stroke of genius. Did you ever see anything like it? Let's hear it for the cake!"

The subsequent cheering is long-lasting and generous. When Malcolm lays a hand gently on the shoulder of my lavender gauze cape, I dare to look up and see that his smile is as genuine as the applause. He holds up his other hand to stay the noise, and turns back to me to continue.

"Victoria, sweetheart, this wonderful cake, with its incredible edible stone effect, just goes to show what a perfect match we are. As if we didn't know that already."

Even more thunderous applause gives me the excuse I need to release the tears that have been welling up in my eyes ever since my sisters brought out the cake. Uninhibited, they pour down my cheeks, but I don't care, knowing everyone will take them as a sign of my utter happiness. Which they are.

Malcolm sits down, leans across to me, and whispers, "Actually, we're going to Venice, but that just felt like the right thing to say."

At that moment I know I have indeed found my perfect match, and that's what will really matter, long after my appalling cake has been toyed with and crumbled and sneaked, largely uneaten, into seventy-three empty pizza boxes.

4

Snoring

At first, Alex's snoring had seemed endearing, providing a rich source of comedy for Louise to share with friends. Describing his extraordinary repertoire of sounds and rhythms allowed her to deflect more personal questions about their bedroom activities that she preferred not to answer. Joking also allowed her to make light of his only irritating habit. Apart from that, he was a real catch.

When Louise and Alex had announced their engagement on the anniversary of their first date, their friends and family had showered them with sincere congratulations and good wishes. There had been only one dissenter: Louise's best friend. Trina had never laughed as loudly or as long as other friends at Louise's impressions of Alex's snoring habit. She saw it as a still invisible fault line in the couple's otherwise perfect relationship; a not-so-silent harbinger of discomfort to come.

On Louise's hen night, Trina, unable to contain her concerns, had taken her friend to one side in the ladies' toilets. They had stood side by side, applying lipstick in front of the spotlit wall mirror.

Louise slicked on a shiny peach that shimmered over her unflickering smile, echoing the gold strands woven into in her short satin dress. The matte purple of Trina's lipstick provided the only splash of colour in her all-black outfit.

"Thanks for being such a sport about the bridesmaids' outfits," Louise said. "You're going to look gorgeous in silver."

The silver had been a hard-won compromise between Louise's preference for lilac over Trina's habitual black.

"Here. These are for you. My gift to my bridesmaid." Louise pulled out from her bag a small purple card bearing diamond and gold earrings in the shape of stars. She'd chosen them to look pretty and feminine, while also appealing to Trina's interest in magic and white witchery.

Trina held out her hand to take them, and examined them under the spotlight above the vanity mirror. "Thanks, Louise, they're gorgeous. They must have cost a fortune. But I'll only accept them if you let me give you something in return."

"But you've already given us your wedding present. We loved your crystal candlesticks. And the trough of medicinal herb plants. And the CD of whale songs. You mustn't spend any more on us."

Louise knew that Trina's New Age shop in the hippy town of Glastonbury was barely breaking even due to too much competition and a glut in the local market. She suspected the gifts had served time in the "reduced" basket on Trina's shop counter, but she didn't mind. It was the thought that counted, not the cost.

Trina shook her head. "I want to give you advice about Alex's snoring. You've got to fix it, or it'll drive you nuts. You need to train him out of it. Or you could hypnotise yourself so either you don't notice it, or you find his awful racket appealing. I can hypnotise you now if you like. I've just finished a course with Gawain, who runs the shop next door to mine. Would you like that? I've been dying to practise on someone."

Hastily Louise shook her head.

"Sounds a bit dangerous to me. Suppose it goes wrong? I don't want to end up walking down the aisle under the illusion that I'm a chicken, or stabbing Alex with the wedding cake knife."

Trina shrugged. "Okay, on your head be it. Or rather, your eardrums."

Ignoring Trina's pointed stare, Louise turned on the tap to rinse her hands under a gentle trickle of water.

As they headed to the honeymoon suite in the Excalibur Hotel, where they'd held their reception, Louise and Alex agreed that the day's events had gone like a dream. Everyone appeared to have had a wonderful time; the church choir sang like angels; the sun shone; the catering was fabulous; and the dance band got everyone up on the marquee floor, even the grandparents. Their special day had felt positively enchanted.

"Now it's the first night of the rest of our lives," beamed Alex. He swept Louise off her feet and carried her across the threshold of their bedroom. "I hope you haven't spent all your energy on the dance floor. Let's start as we mean to go on."

Two hours later, Louise lay silently awake as Alex snored contentedly at her side. She tried not to think of Trina's last-minute warning. Had jealousy triggered her surprising outburst? No, Trina was a good soul, and her intentions sincere. But hypnotism! Louise let out a laugh. Even for Trina and her mystical ways, that was going a bit far.

Unable to settle, Louise sat up, flipped the top pillow to access the cool side, and thumped it into a bow-tie shape. Muffling both ears at once was the best way she'd found yet of dealing with Alex's incessant snoring. It seldom worked.

"Let's start as we mean to go on," he had said. A vision of spending every night for the next fifty years wearing her pillow as ear-muffs opened up before her.

Louise threw back the duvet tetchily and swung her feet to the floor. Perhaps she was just dehydrated after all the champagne. A glass of water might help her sleep.

She drained the first glass in the bathroom, then returned to the bed with a refill. Lying down beside Alex, she pulled the duvet over her head. Too stuffy. She flung it back again, sighed, and clasped her hands behind her head.

The snoring wouldn't be as bad if it wasn't such a hideous noise. Louise fiddled with the pillow, wondering what the lump was at the back of her neck. Holding her hands aloft for inspection, she saw the black leather bracelet that Trina had slipped onto her wrist as they left the reception.

"It's a one-wish wonder – use it wisely."

Louise hadn't examined the bracelet closely until now. Twisting it round, she discovered the simple, slim leather strap was lightly embossed on the outside with the phases of the moon. Flipping it over, she discovered the legend: "Be careful what you wish for". Louise smiled. Trina always had to have the last word! But it was a sweet gift. Though black, it was delicate, a good compromise between Trina's witchy tastes and Louise's preference for pretty. Louise had often wondered whether Trina would drop the grunge if she ever hooked up with a super chap like Alex.

She rolled onto her side to look at her new husband, feeling calmer as she stroked the soft leather. Really, Alex was very handsome. If it wasn't for his snoring, he'd be perfect. She'd thought of the many ways she'd described it to her friends. The sound of an earthquake, with some of the vibrations too; a monster from Doctor Who with its own ratchetty language, not so scary once you understood it had no evil intentions; the relentless waves on a beach full of concrete pebbles; the waste disposal of that cottage they'd taken for their last girls-only holiday. If only it carried a pleasanter sound, like the gentle flowing of a peaceful Highland stream, or the whale song of Trina's CD, or the dawn chorus…

When Louise awoke in the early hours of the morning, she forgot for a moment where she was. The familiar bedside alarm clock was missing, so was her dressing table and her wardrobe. And hang on, she didn't remember buying these fancy sheets. Then she twigged: the honeymoon suite! Bliss! Six more days of self-indulgence before they returned to work.

But what was that sound? She glanced at the glass of water on the nightstand beside her. Had she left the tap running when she filled it during the night? She could definitely hear running water. She lifted her head from the pillow. Yes, that was running water all right, but the sound wasn't coming from the bathroom. A leaky pipe, perhaps? No, it sounded gentler than that, like a peacefully flowing stream.

She sat up now in bed, adrenaline trickling into her system. Had she woken up to a crisis? Then she realised: the source of the watery noise lay right beside her. Her peacefully sleeping husband, while making all the usual motions of his snoring – juddering jaw, twitching nose – was emitting only the sound of a gentle Highland stream.

Louise's head hit her pillow with a thud. Surely not…

Withdrawing her hands from beneath the duvet to examine the bracelet again, she remembered her friend's enigmatic words: "It's a one-wish wonder. Be careful what you wish for."

Suddenly all became clear. Using the magical powers of Trina's bracelet, Louise had reset Alex's nocturnal effects to mimic a gently trickling stream.

She wondered at the implications. On the plus side, if his snoring ever woke her up in the night again, its gentle sound would send her straight back to sleep.

"Trina, you're a genius!" Louise said aloud.

She nipped to the loo before snuggling back down beside Alex for her anticipated deep and refreshing sleep.

But it was not to be. Every hour or so she was woken by the inexplicable need to go to the bathroom. This affliction was to dog her every night for the rest of her married life, while her husband slumbered peaceful as a baby.

5

An Appetite for Marriage

"My God, that woman was gorgeous," announced Ryan the minute Barney sauntered into the office the night after the firm's Christmas party. "What's she doing with an old man like you? Bit young, isn't she?"

At twenty-three, Ryan was the most junior member of the sales department. He regarded Barney, his boss, as a father figure, with a healthy mixture of warmth, respect, and scorn.

Barney shrugged. "Tessa's two years older than you, mate."

"Ha! Don't you realise that when you're fifty, she'll still be in her thirties? And when you're sixty, she'll be forty-three. Don't you think you'll have a problem keeping up with her?"

On the word "up", he gave Barney a lecherous wink.

"Age is a state of mind, my son. And besides, she is my soul-mate."

Barney's PA Diana sniggered without looking up from her keyboard. "Poor girl's probably young enough to think she can change you. She'll learn."

"Yep, she'll change me all right. Into a happily married man. On May the twenty-third. Save the date. You're all invited."

Organised by the efficient and methodical Tessa, the wedding was as smooth as her long white satin dress. After their honeymoon in the Bahamas, Barney bounced into the office with his confidence not only intact but expanded, following a blissful fortnight laying claim to his new wife. He'd expected work might seem dull after such a wonderful break, but his office routine was enhanced each day by her loving provision of a healthy home-made packed lunch.

Previously Barney's idea of a balanced office lunch had been to choose a different country's cuisine every day of the week. Monday meant McDonalds, Tuesday curry, Wednesday pizza, Thursday Chinese. On Friday, he reverted to type with the classic full English all-day breakfast in the nearest pub, washed down with a pint of Guinness.

Tessa shared Barney's love of international cuisine, but showed a lighter touch. Greek salad, Japanese-style sushi, and French *salade niçoise* were typical surprises in his lunch-box. She sugared the pill of low-fat, low-calorie meals by placing a loving note on the top of each one, an explanatory menu detailing the calorie count in small letters.

On Barney's first day back, Ryan picked up one of his sushi rolls and examined it, as if looking for signs of life. "That'll never keep you going till tea-time. It's no lunch for an active man like you." Ryan assumed that all men shared his youthful enthusiasm for playing five-a-side football after work several times a week.

Diana looked up from the limp green salad trapped in her ancient Tupperware tub. "No, but he can live off his hump."

"Eh?" Ryan looked confused.

Diana patted her own round tummy by way of an explanation.

"He has plenty of spare stores on board. Fat. Isn't it obvious? Tessa's trying to slim him down. Now she's got him, she wants to mould him into her ideal man. She'll want him to be slim like her. Marriages are happiest when both partners are of the same build. Two skinnies or two fatties equal happiness, but one of each is almost always doomed. Didn't you know?"

Barney wasn't listening, too busy trying to pick up a sushi parcel with the chopsticks thoughtfully provided by his wife. It slipped from their uncertain grip and landed with a delicate splat on the tiled floor.

"I give up. This isn't real food. Anyone want anything from McDonald's while I'm there?"

His colleagues shook their heads, and Diana suppressed a wry smile.

"That's the thin end of the wedge," she said, loading a piece of bendy cucumber into her mouth and trying to look as if she was enjoying it. "Or maybe the fat one."

"Go on, Di, set up an office sweepstake," called out George from behind the accounts partition. "Guess his weight by Christmas."

Not wanting to hurt his new wife's feelings, Barney continued to bring to work the packed lunches she so lovingly prepared for him. But instead of eating them, he traded them for favours from his colleagues.

In return for clearing his backlog of filing, Diana claimed a Hawaiian Delight, convinced that the combination of cottage cheese and pineapple had magical fat-reducing powers.

"I'll make your morning coffee every day for a week if you give me your sushi," called out Polly as Barney's latest takeaway wafted essence of vindaloo past her reception desk.

"I wouldn't mind a bit of that Greek salad to liven up my kebab," said Ryan, looking up from the Daily Mirror's sports pages. "Swap you for the news section."

Even the traditional British dishes went down well in the office. The English Country Garden Salad, as Tessa labelled it, was passed around from desk to desk to be admired.

"She carved all these herself," said Barney, proudly holding up a delicate rose-shaped radish and a carrot doing a passable impression of a marigold.

"Now there's a woman with too much time on her hands," said George, who had just wandered into the staff dining room clutching an old ice cream tub, his wife's preferred vehicle for his packed lunch. "Hasn't she got a job to go to?"

He selected a cucumber spiral from the box. It rose like a Slinky with nowhere to go. Barney shook his head.

"No, she gave up her job at Sutton Library when she moved in with me. The commute was much too far."

Diana, looking up from her keyboard, fixed him with the cool gaze of a high court judge. "So, has she worked out yet why her slim-line lunches haven't made you lose any weight?"

"Funnily enough, she did remark last night that she thought it odd. She's blaming stress hormones from the pressure of my job. Stress hormones make me store more calories, apparently, in case I need reserves to go into battle."

"Been sprinkling stress hormones on your double cheeseburgers again?" asked Diana. "You won't get away with that theory for long, not once she's got the confetti out of her hair. You'd better have your excuses ready, or some distraction techniques."

Barney had the decency to look abashed, at least until he reached Pizza Hut.

By the time he returned, bearing a distinctive flat square box, he was looking a little more cheerful. Diana, grazing on his floral-themed salad, moved to make room for him on the sofa. He certainly needed more room than he used to, she reflected. Marital bliss was going to his waistline. She watched him lift the pizza box lid reverentially and rub his hands together in anticipation. Then she noticed a Thornton's carrier bag hanging from his wrist.

"What's in there, pudding?" she asked disdainfully.

"What? Oh no, something much more useful." He slipped the bag off his wrist and held it open to show her the contents. "Look, I'm taking evasive action."

He pulled out a four-page form bearing the local council's logo on its front page. "I called into the library in the High Street on the way back and asked whether they had any vacancies. Apparently one's just come up for a full-time librarian. Perfect opportunity for Tessa, and I could give her a lift to work every day."

He rummaged some more and brought out a violet carton topped by a lavish gold ribbon bow.

"The library's next door to a chocolate shop. She'll never resist it. And if she tells me it's the stress of work that's putting inches on her waist, I'll choose to believe her."

George looked up from a large slab of fruit cake, a regular feature in the ample lunch that his pleasingly plump wife had packed for him every day for the last thirty years.

"Well, if that's not a recipe for a happy marriage, I don't know what is," he observed, retrieving a stray sultana from his tie and popping it in his mouth.

PART III

ENDURING

1

Granted

"If you could kindly chew a fraction louder, they'll be able to hear you next door."

Gary crunches on, then slurps as he runs his large tongue around his lips to lap up any traces of plum jam. Gary hates waste. Strange now to think that his careful attitude towards money was one of the things that made me decide to marry him, seventeen years ago. I thought it would counterbalance my natural extravagance.

He washes down his toast with a loud gulp of tea and sets the empty mug on the wrong side of his plate. I don't know why he does that. It's not as if he's left-handed. As usual, I move it back to the right side of his plate when he departs to pay his usual 7.53am visit to the smallest room.

While he is gone, I pop up to the bathroom to straighten the bathmat, scoop up his pyjamas from the floor, and consign them to the laundry basket.

"Thoughtful of you to make it this easy for me to find your pyjamas after your bath, dear," I murmur through gritted teeth. "And to leave them in a soggy heap for me to pick up. I do so like to feel useful."

Next, I gather up a cluster of wet towels, still warm and fragrant from his early morning dip – as is the array of hairs he's left in the bath.

"If you're going to have wet towels, much better to make them uniformly wet by dropping them in the bath before it's drained. And the fragrance – isn't that my special Christmas bath foam? How lovely to enjoy it second hand."

I blame those little notices he sees in hotels, telling guests to leave used towels in the bath when they need replacing. He pays more attention to those signs than he does to me.

I wring the towels out – no point in washing them after a single use – and hang each one neatly on its own rung of the heated towel rail.

"It's good to be able to cost-justify its purchase."

It beats me how an engineer can be unable to use a towel rail properly, not grasping that a wet towel on top of a dry one doesn't result in two dry towels.

Gary, whistling the 'Hallelujah Chorus' in the downstairs loo, doesn't hear any of this.

When he emerges at 8.03am, he throws the newspaper, open at the half-completed crossword puzzle, down on the table. The top right hand corner of the paper wicks up the milk spilled from his All-Bran. Then he buttons up his jacket, seizes his briefcase from the sideboard, and marches to the front door, switching off the lights to leave the kitchen and me in the dark. As he heads for the front door, I follow behind, grabbing my handbag and packed lunch from the hall table. I let him do the manly thing of locking the door behind us. He has his uses.

We part company, as usual, at the end of the front garden path. Gary turns right to head for the railway station, and I take a left for the bus stop. I always find this parting of the ways refreshing, opening up time and space ahead of me that will be all mine, and I take the first few steps with gusto. We pace apart with our backs to each other, as if about to fight a duel – there are days when I would really like to turn and fire a pistol, especially when he's neglected to flush the loo. I'd be quicker on the draw and more accurate than him.

After about ten paces, Gary gives his usual little whistle, as if calling a dog to heel. My teeth clenched with resentment, I turn my head to look back at him over my shoulder. He flashes me a broad toothpaste-shiny smile, and I remember from this distance how handsome he still is to strangers.

"Missing you already, love!" he cries. "Have a wonderful day!"

He blows me a kiss, which I return in spite of myself.

A woman aged about twenty is walking towards me, beaming.

"You lucky thing!" she says in a low voice. "I wish my boyfriend loved me that much."

I shrug, blush, and turn the corner, knowing that, despite all Gary's irritating habits, I will be glad enough to see him again this evening when we both get home from work.

2

Cook's Perks

Martin

Throughout our married life, Barbara's cooked certain dishes for certain occasions. As all of them are delicious, that's fine by me.

Take our wedding anniversary, which happens to be today. The twenty-seventh, in case you're wondering. I know she'll be making *coq au vin* and a sponge cake filled with dairy cream. I also know I'll be picking up a big bunch of roses from the florist's by the station on the way home, same as I do every year. There's not much room left for surprises in our marriage, but I reckon it's safe to stick with the roses.

Barbara

It's not as unoriginal as it might sound to recreate our wedding meal for each anniversary, because, like our marriage, the recipe has been evolving and improving over the years. Gradually we've been able to afford better quality ingredients.

Tonight's dish will be the best yet: a beautiful free-range chicken and some lovely organic button mushrooms and shallots. These days we can even afford to cook with the same quality wine that we'd serve with the meal, just as the top chefs say you should.

It hasn't always been like this. When both the kids were little, I made do with cheap chicken wings, and we couldn't afford decent wine. One year I substituted Ribena – not my best idea. Another year, I bought whipped cream, reduced for a quick sale, which made the sponge taste cheesy. Still, we've always been happy to celebrate another year together.

Martin

Barbara's always been a meticulous cook. She's amassed hundreds of recipes, but says she's still looking for the perfect cookery book. The kids keep telling her to write one. They tuck into her food when they visit, and she always sends them back to their flats with leftovers in old ice-cream tubs. Last year our son bought her a huge set of Tupperware boxes for Christmas. I think she was pleased.

Barbara

I enjoy cooking for just the two of us these days. It's much easier when you don't have to accommodate children's fads, or worry about giving them a balanced diet. Avoiding germs used to be such an issue, too. I was very relieved when the kids outgrew the need for sterilised bottles, and I no longer had to avoid giving them risky foods such as peanuts and whole grapes.

Martin will eat anything I put in front of him, so I can cook to please myself now, and I do.

Martin

Barbara's much more relaxed about her cooking these days, which makes mealtimes a pleasanter experience all round. When the kids were small, she'd get anxious about hygiene. If anything fell on the floor, she'd put it straight in the bin. I thought we should get a dog to hoover up the bits, but she was worried that its poo would send the kids blind. I never did tell her about the time I saw Marcus, aged two, eat a big juicy worm in the garden. I just crossed my fingers and hoped he'd be okay. He was, of course.

Barbara

Once they started school, I had less control over what the children ate, what with school dinners and playdates and teas at friends' houses. It took me a while to succumb to the five-second-rule philosophy that they brought home from the playground – any food falling on the floor is still safe to eat if you pick it up in less than five seconds. That rule must have saved me a fortune over time, both in wasted food and in bottles of disinfectant. I never applied it to my own food, though, only to Martin's and the kids'.

Martin

When I first started seriously courting Barbara, my dad said to me, "Take a good look at her mother, because that's who she'll turn into in twenty years' time". Barbara's mother was a professional chef before she gave up work to get married, and her dad always seemed contented, so I knew I was on to a good thing.

Barbara

When my mum taught me to cook, she told me about the concept of "cook's perks". The way she explained it was this. If you're filling a sponge cake with dairy cream, and you press the top layer down, you run your finger round the edge to neaten the finish, then lick the excess cream off. This concept is cousin to that other great kitchen maxim: "What the eye doesn't see, the heart doesn't grieve over". When I'm preparing sausages, for example, and one of them looks a bit greenish, I give that one to Martin instead of myself. He never guesses, so we're both happy.

Martin

Barbara's a generous cook, always giving me the lion's share. What husband wouldn't be happy with that? I know quite a few blokes whose wives don't cook at all, or they are so bad at cooking that the husbands have to do it all themselves. They claim it relaxes them at the end of a day's work, and gives them the excuse to plan a menu comprising their favourite foods. I can't see it myself. In any case, what I like best is whatever Barbara cooks.

Barbara

Jointing a beautiful plump organic corn-fed chicken this afternoon is pure joy. *Coq au vin* doesn't get any better than this. Then I split each layer of the sponge cake, still warm from the oven, using my favourite knife, a wedding present which still serves me well.

I top and tail the tiny pearl onions and baby Chantenay carrots, before deciding to sample the *vin*. It smells divine. Good thing I've bought three bottles of the stuff. This year, it's so posh it has a proper cork rather than a screw top. In the olden days, I never felt tempted to have a glass of the ninety-nine pence bottles of Hirondelle. It doesn't matter that I've just knocked the chicken pieces all over the floor. Never mind, I can easily pick them up again. Five-second-rule.

Martin

Barbara loves my roses, as usual. She always says you can't beat a nice bunch of red roses. Over dinner we laugh at the memory of the years when we were so hard up that I bought plastic roses from Woolworths, or persuaded the kids to make fakes flowers out of sweet wrappers and pipe cleaners.

This year's *coq au vin* is the best I've ever tasted. I joke that, like the wine and our marriage, it improves with age. We polish off the whole of the dairy cream sponge between us, along with the last bottle of wine. (Good thing Barbara had the foresight to buy two.)

Delicious. It's all been absolutely delicious.

Barbara

The roses and the *coq au vin* and the cake and the roses, they've all been bloody lovely. But why is the floor where the ceiling ought to be? I need to go to the bathroom now, but I can't remember where it is, or where I've put my legs.

Martin

Poor Barbara, what a shame after all her hard work to be so sick. It's not the waste of food or money that I care about, just Barbara. I panicked when she fell and cracked her head on the side of the bath before passing out, but the paramedics were very understanding.

In A&E they took some specimens, of which Barbara unfortunately still had plenty. They said they'd test them for food poisoning. I said I didn't think it could be that, because we'd both eaten exactly the same things. They suggested her resistance might be weaker if she'd had less exposure to germs than me, but I didn't see how that could be the case.

They've kept her in overnight for observation. If she's in for longer, I'll take the roses in to cheer her up. Now it's 2am and she's asleep, and the nurses are telling me to go home to grab some sleep. I might just polish off the last of the *coq au vin* before I go to bed. I'm curiously peckish.

3

The New Coat

"I'd like a new coat for the wife, please – one that doesn't make her sweat."

For a moment, I thought the tall, thin middle-aged customer in front of me was trying to make a joke. In spite of Outdoor Adventures' in-store training on how to respond to customer enquiries, I couldn't stop myself staring at him for a moment before I got a grip and replied.

"Certainly, sir, do you happen to know her size, please?"

A shorter, slender woman with a tight greying perm was standing beside him. I had assumed she wasn't his wife because he spoke as if his wife were absent.

"I'm size eight, dear," the woman piped up with a nervous smile.

"The wife's size eight," repeated her husband. "Though I think we'll go for size ten, in case she wants to wear a cardigan underneath it. Yes, size ten will do nicely."

"Size ten," she echoed quietly.

"Do you have a specific budget in mind, sir?" I tried to make eye contact directly with the woman. Despite her meek demeanour, her electric blue eyes shone, bright, intelligent and warm, above her rosy cheeks, but not at me.

"No more than sixty pounds, thank you," replied her husband straight away. "Nothing cheap, nothing extravagant. Something serviceable and built to last. Something to keep her cosy, whatever the weather."

I led them towards the rail of hiking jackets on special offer.

"I recommend our Somerset range." Selecting one in a kingfisher shade, I thought the colour would draw attention to the woman's beautiful eyes. I held it up against myself to go through the routine of showing off its features, like a flight attendant demonstrating a life preserver.

"The peach-finish of the Somerset range makes it soft and warm to the touch, yet it has a surprisingly tight weave that wards off wind chill."

I stroked the surface appreciatively before pulling down the zip.

"The sturdy zip opens easily, even when you're wearing gloves, and the adjacent row of snap fasteners provides extra insulation."

I glanced up at the woman to gauge whether she was impressed. If not, I'd switch to the chunkier Dorset range.

"But will it make her sweat?" asked her husband, his voice unmuted by any respect for her finer feelings. I heard guffaws from a couple of young girls browsing ski-pants nearby and shot them a black look, as if to say "Come on, we're all sisters here".

"The material is fully breathable, sir, ensuring a consistently comfortable and healthy body temperature."

He lunged forward to raise a sleeve, and touched the pair of eyelets beneath the right armpit.

"Ah, ventilation holes. Excellent."

His wife continued to smile sweetly.

"I don't like the colour," he objected. "Blue is for boys."

"Really? I thought the kingfisher blue was a perfect match for your wife's stunning eyes."

I shoot her a look of approval, and she let out a tiny twittering laugh. "Ooh, I say!"

"Well, we prefer pink," said her husband. He selected from the rail a coat the colour of ripe raspberries, a shade I'd expressly avoided for fear of drawing attention to the woman's florid complexion. "Yes, that's the ticket. Let's try that one on, shall we, dear?"

His wife immediately slipped out of her thundercloud-grey plastic raincoat, which I took to leave her hands free. With a chivalry that surprised me, her husband removed the pink jacket from its hanger and held it open for her. She turned her back and slid her arms into the sleeves. He placed his hands on her shoulders to spin her round to face him again. When she fumbled to fasten the zip, he gently pushed her hands aside and did it for her, drawing the tag right up to the high neck of her flowery pink cotton blouse. Then he snapped closed all the stud fasteners and tied up the drawstring on the hood. She looked ready for an Arctic expedition.

I continued my patter. "If you're planning to hike anywhere especially cold, you may like to invest in the optional fleece liner, easily fastened in place by internal studs, and available separately for just nineteen ninety-nine."

I interpreted the pat he gave her hooded head as a buying signal.

"Oh no, I don't think a lining will be necessary," he replied. "We're not going hiking. Only shopping, visiting the library, that sort of thing. I just want to protect the wife from the elements."

Perhaps she might not want to be protected, I mused as he began investigating the multiple pockets, an integral feature of the Somerset range. Maybe she'd like to feel spring rain on her flesh; to have the cobwebs blown away by fresh breezes; to display more of her skin than her hands and face. Wondering whether she might be Vitamin D deficient, I surreptitiously checked her calves for signs of rickets.

After fastening and unfastening every available pocket, he stowed the hood away in the concealed pouch behind the collar. Then he stood back to admire his handiwork, like a sculptor deciding whether he'd completed his latest creation – only his Venus de Milo had a need for sleeves.

"There!" he said, smiling for the first time since he'd entered the shop. His lean face was suddenly suffused with an unexpected warmth. "Pretty as a picture."

To my surprise, he bent down to give his wife a tender kiss on the lips, making her flush with pleasure. I couldn't have been more startled if he'd bestowed a kiss on me. As he straightened to his full height, I noticed he too was pinker of complexion and breathing a little faster.

In spite of my professional training, I was swayed by his enthusiasm. "You look lovely," I told her. "Will you take it?"

"Ooh, yes please!" exclaimed the wife. "May I keep it on?"

Her request reminded me of shoe-shopping trips with my mum when I was a little girl.

Her husband took her plastic mac from me and folded it neatly. After tucking it inside the capacious pocket of his car-coat, he patted it, as if to assure his wife that he was taking good care of her property.

As I led them towards the till, he reached into his trouser pocket and produced his wallet, peering into the note section. "I'm afraid I'm ten pounds short. I'll leave the wife here while I pop to the cashpoint next door."

"We can take payment by card, sir, to save you the trouble."

He shook his head. "Oh no, thank you very much. I like to control my money."

He turned to his wife. "You stay here, dear. I won't be gone long."

Take your time, I thought. Give the woman a break.

I half expected him to produce a collar and lead, and tie her to the counter before he departed. She simply beamed and nodded in obedience, then watched him stride out of the shop.

"It is a lovely coat, isn't it?" she said shyly. "I'm very pleased with it."

"Yes, it is, and it suits you," I lied. I didn't want to burst her bubble of contentment, and, after all, I had just made a sale.

Then she leaned forward conspiratorially. "I'm a very lucky woman. My husband really looks after me." I noticed her glancing pityingly at my bare left hand.

I pressed the button to make the till drawer spring open. "Yes. Yes, I can see that he does. Lucky you."

A moment later he returned and placed six ten-pound notes onto the counter. As I fed the notes, still warm from the cash machine, under the spring-loaded clip in the tenner drawer, she slipped her slender hand into his. He gave it a gentle squeeze of affection.

"I think we've got a good deal there, dear," he assured her, then, looking directly at me, added, "Yes, that'll see her out."

It was to her that I handed the till receipt. "You may like to know, madam, that we offer a no-quibble returns policy. At Outdoor Adventures, we do understand that sometimes things can seem attractive in the shop, but don't always have the same appeal when you get them home. You can change your mind and bring it back for an exchange or full refund, any time in the next thirty days. The choice is yours."

The woman turned to look up at her husband, who answered for her.

"Thank you, miss, but I'm sure that won't be necessary. We're perfectly happy as we are."

And do you know, though his attitude flew in the face of my feminist principles, I'm sure he was speaking the truth.

4

False Economies

Today's deposit tips my balance to over five thousand pounds. That's more than enough to cover the cost of my secret surprise. I hug the building society pass book to my chest, closing my eyes with excitement at my achievement. My husband Brian knows nothing about it, nor how I plan to spend it – yet.

As soon as I get home, I tuck the book back into its secret hiding place: the duster drawer in the kitchen. I know my secret will be safe from Brian there.

Even so, I can't help wishing I could see the look on Brian's face when he realises I've saved that much money without his knowledge. You see, we've always had a joint bank account. Brian assumed we'd have one as soon as we got married, and I went along with him without thinking. It's what women did in those days.

"A joint bank account is a symbol of your mutual trust," my best friend Pamela had advised me. "If you can see where all your joint income's going, you'll always know he's not spending money on some bit on the side."

If I'd been married to Pamela's Ed, I'd have wanted that reassurance too. But my Brian wasn't the straying type, and I don't think he wanted a joint account to keep tabs on me. He just liked the idea of marrying a fluffy bunny who couldn't get her head around household economics.

I may have encouraged him to develop that opinion by allowing him to pick up the tab when we were courting. It made him feel manly.

After our wedding, I was happy to let Brian manage our money, even when I was earning more than him. Our salaries played leapfrog until I gave up work to have our children. I didn't take much notice when he held forth at our monthly family money conferences, reconciling our bank account against copious cheque stubs and rarer deposit counterfoils. I simply accepted the budget he imposed, which included a decent housekeeping allowance.

After a year or two, I realised that, provided my outgoings didn't exceed that housekeeping allowance, Brian would never ask how I'd spent it. The total on the bank statement for a weekly big shop at the local supermarket would be proof enough that I'd done my bit for the financial wellbeing of my family. He never asked to check the till receipts to see what I'd bought. On the other hand, if I spent money in any other shops -- boutiques, hairdressers, beauticians – I had to justify the expense.

I soon worked out that I could easily pass the monthly test in spirit, while cheating wildly. If I needed new tights, I could slip a few pairs into the supermarket trolley and pass them off as part of the grocery bill. I was overjoyed when supermarkets, once purveyors only of food, began to diversify, adding make-up, clothing, handbags, jewellery, videos, DVDs, and all kinds of other non-food items to their shelves.

I also quickly learned that Brian had no concept of the price difference between own brand and proprietary products. Provided he never saw the packaging, which I ensured he never did, he couldn't tell between an Asda custard cream and a Huntley and Palmers. That netted me about fifty pence per packet.

Or should I say profited? Because it was only a small step from there to convince Brian that I should pay cash for our groceries, on the basis that it made me more aware of how much I was spending. After that, the discrepancy between the actual bill and the housekeeping budget was all mine.

Supermarket shopping started to feel like a competitive sport, with my financial wits pitched against Brian's. I developed plenty of tactics to make sure I always won. When glass storage jars were on special offer at Tesco, I snapped up a dozen, decanting own brand staples into them to pass off as top of the range products. When items were reduced for quick sale, I peeled off the lower priced stickers before I got home, making it look as if I'd paid the original price.

At first, I spent my profit on the kids, buying things that Brian would never countenance, and for which there was no allowance in our household budget: Mr Whippy ice-creams in the park on the way home from school; children's rides on mechanical machines at the supermarket checkout; comics chosen for the tacky plastic free gifts sellotaped to their front covers. It was much easier to pay for such things without asking Brian for extra cash, thus averting many a tiresome and unnecessary lecture on money management.

When the children went away to university, it gave me great pleasure to slip a tenner into my weekly letter to them. I could tell them to blow it on a treat, without

Brian accusing me of spoiling them or stopping them from standing on their own two feet. Even better, although my grocery bill plummeted during term-time, Brian never thought to reduce my monthly housekeeping budget when the children were away, or even when they'd left home for good.

Now the kids are both gainfully employed and financially independent, I'm free to spend all my housekeeping profit on myself, but I don't feel the need. I've plenty of material things, and I'm at the stage where I get a bigger buzz from chucking stuff out than acquiring more. I'm not as bothered about keeping up with fashion, and I've plenty of favourite old clothes that I'm happy to wear.

So for the last few years, instead of spending my housekeeping profit, I've been stashing it away in a secret building society account. Brian would be incredulous if he knew how well I've done. After all, I've saved more than he has in the equivalent time, for all his meticulous budgeting.

Now and again, when I'm alone, I get my building society passbook out to look at it and remind myself of how clever I've been. I wonder what Brian will say when I tell him, just before our golden wedding anniversary, that I've saved enough to take us off on a luxury cruise. It's the least we deserve after a lifetime of financial caution.

But in the meantime, whenever Brian's parsimony gets me down, it comforts me to know that, with thirty days' notice to the building society, I could buy a one-way ticket to anywhere in the world, leaving Brian to wonder how I paid for it.

Fortunately for Brian, so far my anger has always abated by day twenty-six of the notice period. In the meantime, the interest continues to accrue.

91

5

The Butterfly Clip

Arthur didn't enjoy supermarket shopping, but he had no choice now that his wife Minnie could no longer do it on her own. In fact, neither could he. Provided they each remembered to take their walking sticks, together they could just about manage it.

"What a team!" Arthur used to say, always one to put a positive spin on life. A team for over sixty years now.

They'd progress around the supermarket together, Arthur with a traditional wooden walking stick in his right hand, Minnie holding in her left a lighter aluminium one. With their free hands, they'd push the trolley between them. Minnie selected the goods and Arthur, whose grip was stronger, took her chosen items from the shelf and placed them in the trolley.

Although the local supermarket was relatively small, their weekly circuit took them an hour. Their slow walking pace was only part of the problem. The other challenge was the amount of choice. Almost every purchase triggered a discussion.

"Strawberries or raspberries for tea tonight, dear?"

"Oh, strawberries for me, dear. Those raspberry seeds get under my plate."

"Look at those new spring lamb chops, don't they look nice and plump?"

"A bit too chewy, don't you think, Arthur? Let's have some minced lamb for a lovely shepherd's pie instead. Same flavour, less chewing."

"How about a spot of salad for lunch tomorrow? Nice and summery with a bit of cheese or maybe a little *quiche Lorraine*."

"Ooh, no, put that cucumber back, Arthur. You know what it does to you."

By the time they arrived at the checkout after all their deliberations, they would barely have covered the bottom of the trolley with the amount of food they needed to satisfy their small appetites.

Each week, as Arthur transferred the goods from the checkout counter to their wheeled shopping basket, he tutted to himself at the nature of the food that lay before him. So much soft chewy readily-digestible pap, the only kind of food that would pass muster with their worn-out digestive systems and unreliable false teeth. They might as well buy baby food. Poor old souls, he'd think. This is the autumn of our lives.

Then, patiently watching his wife as she fumbled for the right money in her ancient Harris Tweed purse, he'd glimpse the aged diamanté tortoiseshell butterfly clip pinning back her wispy cotton-white hair. It was the first gift he'd given her, all those years ago when they were courting.

Just for a moment, the supermarket checkout would disappear. Instead he was back in the old orchard by the stream, in his youth when it was never any season but summer. Lying beside him was Minnie, the sunshine sparkling on the butterfly clip in her thick dark curls, as they held hands and crunched on scrumped red apples.

As Minnie accepted the till receipt from the cashier, he'd catch her eye and give her a cheeky wink, which made her blush. Transaction completed, they'd pull their heavy wheeled basket behind them down to the supermarket café. Over a restorative cup of tea, they'd sit together, saying little, perfectly content.

A NOTE TO YOU,
THE READER

Thank you for reading *Marry in Haste*. If you've enjoyed it, please consider leaving a review on Amazon, mentioning it on social media, or recommending it to any friends who might enjoy it. New reviews and recommendations make my day!

If you'd like to be among the first to know about my new books and events, to read my blog, or to send me a message, please visit my author website: www.authordebbieyoung.com. If you join my mailing list, you can claim a free ebook of another short story collection. You'll also find me on Twitter as @DebbieYoungBN, and my author Facebook page is www.facebook.com/AuthorDebbieYoung.

With very best wishes
Debbie Young
January 2016

ACKNOWLEDGEMENTS

I am deeply grateful to the following friends who kindly beta read this collection before it was published: Lucienne Boyce, Mari Howard, Karen Inglis, Micheline Munro, Betsy Talbot, and Shay Tressa DeSimone. Their wisdom, advice and ideas helped make this a much better book, as did the final polish added by my excellent and always dependable editor, Alison Jack. Thanks also to everyone who listened patiently as I reported on the progress of the book, making encouraging noises and laughing at my jokes along the way.

Finally, I should thank my parents for providing such a wonderful role model of marriage, and my husband for his often unwitting inspiration.

OTHER FICTION BY DEBBIE YOUNG

Quick Change

Tiny Tales of Transformation

"I loved these stories. Sly, witty, surprising, and the twists are genuine twists. The characterisation is lovely, very deft and economical. They make domesticity look edgy, sometimes dangerous, but they are also life-affirming."

Lucienne Boyce

Stocking Fillers

Twelve Short Stories for Christmas

"Funny, thoughtful, surprising, heartwarming. A delightful celebration of Christmas that will get you in the festive spirit."

Rebecca Lang